A PICT

At 6:21 a.m. the sun began to rise over the sweet little town of Peaceful Pines.

At 7:34 A.M. the sky cleared. It was going to be another picture-perfect spring day.

At 8:00 A.M. the town square's water sprinklers slowly spun into motion, spraying the lawns with bright blue slime.

At 8:01 A.M. the slime splattered against one of the park benches, where a young girl and a ghost lay sleeping.

They were both having bad dreams.

But their real nightmare was just beginning. . . .

BOOKS BY B.J. SPECTER

Beetlejuice #1: Beetlejuice For President

Beetlejuice #2: Lydia's Scream Date

Beetlejuice #3: Rock 'N' Roll Nightmare

Beetlejuice #4: Twisted Tours

Available from MINSTREL BOOKS

Each had his weird, ugly face in the center. Lydia rolled her eyes.

"But seriously, Lyds," he went on, "I've got a plan that would make us rich."

"No way," Lydia said quickly. "I've learned the hard way about your get-rich-quick schemes. They're only good if you want to get-in-big-trouble-quick."

"This is different," the spirit assured her.

"Anyway, your schemes are always crooked."

Beetlejuice gaped at her, showing off his crooked green teeth. "Crooked? Ouch!" His body bent into hundreds of crooked angles. "That hurts! C'mon, babes, let me in and we'll talk. Puh-leease."

"Okay," Lydia said finally, crossing her arms. "Beetlejuice, Beetlejuice, Beetlejuice."

The ghost jumped into the room and straightened his black tie. "Thanks, you're quite a *ghoul*."

"Now what's the idea this time?"

Beetlejuice grinned slyly. "Travel."

"Travel?"

"Tourists."

"Tourists? Beetlejuice, why don't you just tell me the plan and stop—"

"We sell tours down in the Neitherworld for

creatures who want to see the real world," Beetlejuice replied smugly.

"Are you out of your mind?"

Beetlejuice's brain popped right out of his head. "No. Why?"

"Who would lead these tours?"

"You would, of course."

"No way."

"But you'd be the best tour guide ever," said Beetlejuice. "Who could I ever get who would be as good as you?"

"Don't waste your time buttering me up. The answer is no."

"But Lydia, the creatures will be so disappointed. All they want is to get a peek at the way you people live. And all I want is to bring a little sunshine into their dreary Neitherworld lives. And bring thousands of dollars into my pocket.

"And *your* pocket," he quickly added. "I'll pay you—" He fingered the Beetlejuice bills in his hands. "Ten dollars a tour."

Lydia snorted. "Very generous. You get thousands of dollars for doing nothing and I get ten dollars for doing all the work."

"Twenty?"

"Look, Beetlejuice, Peaceful Pines already has a

ghost. You. And you cause enough trouble for the whole town. Who knows what kind of trouble I'd get in if I let loose a whole batch of you guys."

"Trouble? From tourists? What trouble? They'll snap a few photos, buy a few souvenirs, and head back home."

"I'll see you later," Lydia said, pointing to the mirror.

"Wait!" Beetlejuice dropped to his knees. "You've got to be my tour guide. Pleasey, pleasey, pleasey?"

Lydia shook her head.

Fountains of chocolate sauce poured off Beetlejuice's head. "Pretty please with chocolate sauce and a" — His head turned shiny red and a little stem sprouted out of his forehead— "a cherry on top?"

"Sweet dreams, Beetlejuice."

The ghost grabbed Lydia by the ankle. "I'm begging you. Without you, I can't get the creatures into Peaceful P—"

He stopped midsentence. Lydia was staring down at him. He grinned broadly. "I mean, they won't want to go without a great tour guide like yourself."

But Lydia wasn't paying attention. "Wait a

minute." She snapped her fingers. "Why didn't I think of this before?" She took a hammer and shattered her vampire bank. She counted out the change. Two dollars and forty-nine cents.

"Not even close," said Beetlejuice. "The CD costs twelve dollars and ninety-nine cents. And a CD player costs around two hundred dollars."

"I know!" Lydia said. Then she did a double-take. "Wait a minute. How did you know that's what I wanted?"

Beetlejuice giggled.

"You planted that CD there, didn't you? Just to try to get me to agree to your crazy plan!"

Beetlejuice howled.

"Well, it won't work. You can't trick me, Beetlejuice. I'm going to make my own money. And not with your crazy tourists!"

The next afternoon, when Lydia got home from school, she found her stepmother on a ladder. Delia was painting skyscrapers on the wall of the master bedroom. "Mom," Lydia said, "what's Mrs. Wallaby's number? I'm going to take that baby-sitting job after all."

Delia slid all the way down the ladder. "You're going to what?"

Lydia copied down the number and hurried to

her room. Baby-sitting might be awful, but getting that CD player would make up for it. The one thing she *had* to be careful about was not saying Beetlejuice's name three times, so he couldn't get in and interfere. She could just imagine what he'd do to spoil her plans. She opened her door.

Beetlejuice lay sprawled on her bed, twiddling his thumbs.

"How did you get in?" Lydia gasped.

"I never left. I slept in the cellar."

"The cellar? Isn't that cold and dirty?"

"It was," agreed Beetlejuice. "Fantastic!"

Lydia turned to go.

"Hey! Where are we off to now?"

"*I'm* going baby-sitting. You're going home." Lydia pointed to her mirror.

"Aw, come on," he said. "I can help baby-sit." He was now wearing a diaper, sucking his thumb, and sitting. "See? Baby sit."

"I get it." She pointed again. "*Now*, Beetlejuice."

She waited until he had stepped into the mirror before she headed for the phone. Now she was rid of him for sure.

But what Lydia didn't know was that Beetlejuice still hadn't left. He had kept one foot in her

room. As soon as she turned her back, he tiptoed back into the room.

Lydia picked up the receiver.

"*I* know," schemed Beetlejuice. "I'll bug her phone!"

Instantly, he turned himself into a tiny bug. He jumped into Lydia's ear as she dialed Mrs. Wallaby.

"Hello?" Mrs. Wallaby answered.

The black-and-white striped bug listened carefully. And he heard Lydia say, "Three fifty-nine Oak Lane. Got it. I'll be there at seven sharp."

Lydia hung up the phone. Great. She had a job. She would make the money in no time.

The CD player would be hers.

Best of all, Beetlejuice couldn't interfere, even if he wanted to.

Because Beetlejuice didn't know the address.

CHAPTER TWO

TROUBLE COMES IN THREES

OAK LANE TURNED OUT TO BE A SHADY, QUIET STREET. Of course, in Peaceful Pines there weren't any noisy ones.

Lydia rang the bell. Mrs. Wallaby opened the door and smiled out at her. Her three identical sons were clinging to her skirts. "This is Timmy, Jimmy, and Simmy," she said, patting three little boys with blond hair and blue eyes.

The triplets all said, "Hello, Lydia," at the same time. Mrs. Wallaby smiled broadly. "They love you! Oh, I'm sure everything is going to work out just fine."

At that same moment, the telephone lines that ran through Peaceful Pines began to hum a little louder than usual. Then they burped. Neither

Lydia nor Mrs. Wallaby nor her sons heard it, but a tiny spirit was traveling through the phone lines. He was making his way from the old Deetz house on the hill to 359 Oak Lane.

"And so the big bad wolf puffed himself up until he was very, very big."

Lydia was in the Wallaby childrens' room, reading the *The Three Little Pigs* to the three little boys as a bedtime story.

The three boys were each tucked into his own small bed. She had to admit, they were kind of cute. Even if they weren't snakes.

Then the phone rang.

"Just a second," Lydia told the boys. "I'll be right back."

She answered the phone, but there was no one there. "That's funny," she said.

"Who was it?" Timmy asked.

Jimmy's eyes grew large with panic. "Was it the big bad wolf?"

Lydia laughed. "Of course not. Wolves can't talk. Unless, of course, they're from the Neitherworld." The three boys looked at her in wonder. "But that's another story," she said quickly. "For another night. Now, where was I? Oh, yes, so the wolf—"

"You mean me?"

A gigantic wolf sprang out of the shadows, his bloody fangs bared.

Timmy, Jimmy, Simmy, and Lydia all screamed. Then the boys ran, still screaming, down the front stairs. The wolf was right behind them every step of the way, nipping at their heels.

At least, they thought he was. But when they got to the living room, the wolf was gone.

Lydia caught up with the crying boys. "It was just your imagination," she said, desperate for an explanation. She knew who was up to his old tricks. But how did he find her? "Look, do you see any wolf?" The little boys refused to look. They also refused to go back upstairs.

"All right," Lydia said finally. "You can watch five minutes of television, but then it's off to bed."

She turned on the TV. It took a moment for the picture to come into focus. They saw a long snout, brown hair, dark gleaming eyes—the wolf!

Lydia snapped off the set. The kids all ran screaming into different parts of the house. Lydia chased after them. "Timmy! Jimmy! Simmy! It's okay, it was just a scary movie! I turned it off! Come back!"

Which was when the voice began booming from *outside* the house. "I'll huff," it howled, "and I'll puff and I'll blow your house down!"

A horrible wind blasted through the open windows. Lydia was blown against the wall. When she recovered, she yelled to the kids, "Down to the basement!"

They all started running for the basement door. They were halfway there when a gigantic wolf paw shot through an open window and made a grab at them. Its claws were sharp as daggers.

"Stop!" shouted Lydia as she screeched to a halt, pulling back the boys just in time. They turned and ran the other way, into the living room. They stopped again. The huge face of the wolf was peering into the living room window. His yellow eyes gleamed. He licked his green buck teeth with a huge black-and-white tongue.

The triplets turned and ran. "Beetlejuice!" Lydia hollered. "Of all the low-down dirty rotten tricks! You're scaring these little boys half out of their—"

The wolf disappeared. Lydia sighed with exhaustion.

It took a few minutes for her to find the boys. She spotted Jimmy, hiding behind the sofa. "There's no wolf," Lydia assured him, squeezing him tight.

She found the second boy hiding underneath the kitchen table. She found the third boy hiding under his bed. And she found the fourth boy hiding behind the bedroom door.

Wait a minute. She had been hired to baby-sit for three boys. Not four.

And one of the boys had yellow eyes.

"Beetlejuice!" she cried. She lunged forward, but the yellow-eyed boy giggled and ducked. Lydia chased him through the kitchen and out of the house. She got tangled up in the clothesline and missed Beetlejuice as he ran back inside.

"Good strong rope for tying up ghosts," Lydia told herself. She marched back inside, dragging the clothesline with her. She tackled the ghost in the den.

"Now I've got you!" Lydia said.

"Let me go!" yelped the blue-eyed boy.

"Uh-oh," Lydia said, looking at the boy's blue eyes. "Who are you?"

"Jim-my," said the boy. His voice cracked in the middle as he started to sob.

Lydia quickly let him go. "Jimmy, sorry! I—"

Just then, another boy ran by. Lydia tripped him. This boy did have yellow eyes. She started tying him up with the clothesline. He was laughing too hard to stop her.

Just then, the front door opened.

"Gee, Lyds," said the boy ghost. "I'd love to stick around, but I'm all *tied up* right now." He guffawed, then disappeared in a flash.

Lydia tried to smile brightly as Mr. and Mrs.

Wallaby walked in the door and saw their babysitter with three hysterical boys.

"Lydia?" Delia called through the locked door of Lydia's bedroom. "I just got off the phone with Mrs. Wallaby. She was yelling something about a big bad wolf and a clothesline. Do you have any idea what she means?"

The doorknob rattled. "Let us in, pumpkin," called her father. "Let's talk about it."

Lydia covered her face with her hands. "I don't want to talk about it!"

Beetlejuice's chuckling face filled the screen. "Give up, tour guide?" he asked her.

Lydia leaped to her feet and spun the vertical control knob. Beetlejuice screamed as he flew up into the top of the set, knocking his head again and again and again.

Then Lydia grabbed today's *Peaceful Times*. As Beetlejuice kept yelping and howling, she turned to the Help Wanted ads. . . .

"Ya ever work in a clothing store before?"

"Oh, yes, lots of times," Lydia told the bald-headed store manager, Mr. Grigsby.

Mr. Grigsby studied her closely, then shrugged. "The thing is, your timing is excellent. My dressing room supervisor just quit, so I'll give you a try."

"Yippee!" Lydia jumped up and down. "I promise you won't regret this, Mr. Grigsby."

"I hope not," Mr. Grigsby said. "We pay every Friday."

Dressing room supervisor! A part-time job at the GYP clothing store! It was all too good to be true. Why, in a month she'd have the $212.99 she needed to buy her own CD player and that funeral CD.

She was still daydreaming happily about her future purchase when she saw the moth. She was in the GYP dressing room. She had been folding sweaters for an hour. The moth was tiny with friendly brown eyes. Lydia gently cupped it in her hands and smiled at the insect.

Suddenly, Mr. Grigsby came running into the dressing room, slapping a flyswatter like mad. "Moths!" he shouted. "Get the moths!"

"What's the problem?" Lydia asked in surprise. "They're just bugs."

"Just bugs?" The manager's eyes bugged out of his head. "*Moths* lay eggs, Lydia, right? And the eggs hatch into larvae. Are you with me so far?"

"Uh-huh."

"Right. And do you know what the larvae eat?" He was pulling at the hair that stuck out on either side of his bald head. "The larvae eat my expensive, trendy, wool GYP shirts, slacks, and sweaters!"

Lydia made a fist around the moth she was holding and gently tucked it under her own sweater. "Don't worry," she said. "There was only one moth, and I caught it."

Mr. Grigsby looked at her as if she were crazy. "One moth?" He flung open the dressing room door. Shoppers were running for their lives. Brown moths swarmed everywhere.

Lydia gasped. Mr. Grigsby ran off waving his flyswatter. "Beetlejuice," Lydia fumed. "I'll get you for this."

It took an hour to shoo out all the moths. And the next afternoon, when Lydia arrived for work, there was a "Closed" sign on the GYP door.

"I'm going out of business," Mr. Grigsby explained tearfully. "Look."

He pointed to the racks of the clothes. The clothes were filled with holes, like Swiss cheese. And Lydia was out of a job.

Thursday morning in Peaceful Pines was sunny and clear. Lydia parked her bike in front of the first house on her new paper route. She pulled a paper out of the sack and prepared to fold it. Then she saw the front page photo. And the photo saw her.

"You just don't know when to quit, do you, pal?" sneered the photo of the ghost. *"OW!"*

Lydia rolled up the newspaper. She cocked her arm and aimed for the Clarkson's front porch.

It was a perfect throw. The paper landed right on the doormat. At least it would have. Instead it stopped an inch off the ground, flew back up in the air, and crashed through the Clarkson's bay window.

Lydia's second paper sailed right through an open kitchen window and bonked Mrs. Manicotti on the back of the head, knocking her face into her bowl of fruit cereal.

The third paper slithered under the Twingles' front door, raced up the stairs, and dunked itself in Tweaky Twingle's fishbowl.

Lydia was fired once again.

Now I'll never get work, and I'll never get money, she told herself glumly as she biked homeward. Suddenly, she heard some music that cheered her up right away. Funeral music.

Out in the middle of the town common, someone was playing an electric organ. The organist had a floppy hat resting on top of the organ for donations. He banged away at the keys, pounding out such mournful classics as "Pushing up the Daisies," and "I'm Cryin' Cause Daddy Didn't Name Me in His Will."

Lydia parked her bike and moved closer, fishing in her pocket for change.

"Thanks, kid," said the organist. Then he turned to face her.

"Beetlejuice! You dirty, rotten—"

The ghost turned into a pile of dirt, then a rotting pile of garbage. "You flatter me," he said.

"Stinker!"

Two fumes of bad odor streamed from the garbage and poured into Beetlejuice's nose. *"I'll* say I'm a stinker," he exclaimed, breathing deeply. "Mmmmm. Delicious."

Lydia stomped off toward her bike.

"You're losing your sense of humor, babes," he called as he returned to his organ-playing self.

"You're not funny," she called without looking back.

"That CD player is yours," Beetlejuice yelled, as he launched back into the funeral music. "All you have to do is lead one tour. Just one. And I'll pay you two hundred and fifteen dollars."

She stopped. How bad could it be to lead one tour? And she *was* desperate.

"Seven nice creatures have already signed up," called Beetlejuice. "You don't want to disappoint seven innocent little creatures, now do you? Lydia? Do you?"

CHAPTER THREE

THE KEY TO THE CITY

BEETLEJUICE WAS DRESSED IN A TUXEDO. He spoke into a microphone, his voice booming. "Lydia Deetz . . . it is my great honor. . . ."

"*SSSSHHHHH!*" Lydia hissed. "You'll wake up my folks."

It was almost midnight. Her parents had gone to sleep at ten.

Beetlejuice ignored her and went on with his presentation. "It is my great honor to present you with the key to the city."

He pulled a large key out of his pocket and handed it to Lydia with a flourish. "Meet Arthur," he said.

"Arthur?" said Lydia.

"You got something against my name?" the key quipped.

Lydia looked closer. It wasn't a key at all. It was a bony creature. It had two eyes and a mouth. The mouth moved.

"What are you staring at?" growled Arthur. "You never saw a talking key before?"

"Arthur is a skeleton key," Beetlejuice explained proudly. "He can change his shape and open any lock in this city. Keep him in your pocket."

Lydia dropped the key into her pocket. "Hey! Who turned out the lights?" she heard Arthur say.

"I don't know, Beetlejuice," she said. "Something tells me this isn't a good idea."

"You're right," agreed the ghost. "It isn't a good idea. It's an *incredible* idea. Now here's your guide hat." He handed Lydia a white cap with a card in front that read "Tour Guide." Then he pinned a large button to her sweater. The button read "Welcome, Neitherworld Tourists. My Name Is Lydia."

"Okay," Beetlejuice said, "we're *ready*." He turned bright red. "I'll go back down and send up the tourists." He headed for the mirror, then paused. "Oh, one last thing. You're going to have to say a special spell to let them in."

"Beetlejuice, I'm beginning to feel awfully nervous about this whole thing. I mean—"

Beetlejuice started playing an organ that had

appeared out of thin air. He was playing a wonderfully sad tune called, "Six Feet Underground."

"This could all be yours," he sang, "plus a CD player, after just one tour. . . ."

Lydia bit her lip. "Okay," she said with a sigh. "What's the spell?"

Beetlejuice fingered his chin slyly. "Just an ordinary sort of chant. Repeat after me. O Monster Tourists—"

"O Monster Tourists—" repeated Lydia.

"Here's your visa."

"Here's your visa."

"You can come," said Beetlejuice slowly.

"You can come," echoed Lydia.

Beetlejuice said the last words fast. "Whenever you pleasa."

"Whenever you pleasa," Lydia repeated without thinking.

"See ya," Beetlejuice cried, and he was gone.

"Uh-oh," thought Lydia. But before she had time to think a single other thought, a new face appeared in her mirror. Well, not a face exactly. It was just two huge lips with eyes on top and skinny hairy legs below. The creature hopped into the room and dropped a traveling bag out of its mouth, onto the floor.

"Who are you?" Lydia asked, shocked.

"BIG MOUTH!" bellowed Big Mouth.

"Quiet!" Lydia whispered.

"I DON'T KNOW HOW TO BE QUIET!" Big Mouth hollered.

"Then don't say a word!" Lydia whispered. "It's late here. You know, late? People are sleeping."

"WHO CARES IF THEY'RE SLEEPING!" Big Mouth screamed. "I'M ON VACATION!"

Lydia tried to close the beast's huge mouth with her hands. But just then another tourist popped out of her mirror.

This creature, at least, looked normal. In fact, she looked a whole lot like Lydia's grandmother. She had gray hair and spectacles and a cardigan sweater. Lydia then noticed her hairy feet. And each foot had twenty toes. Well, what was normal anymore, anyway?

"So this is Earth," the grandmother creature said, snapping a photo. "Why, look! You have a bug collection! And stuffed bats!" The grandmother creature peered through her spectacles at Lydia's horror movie posters. "Mummies, skeletons, monsters," she said in a disappointed voice. "Why, this place is no different than the Neitherworld."

"Oh, don't worry. This isn't typical," Lydia said.

She held out her hand. "I'm your guide, Lydia."

"Call me Grandmother."

Suddenly, there was a blinding flash. A creature with what looked like a thousand eyes leaped into the room. There was a second blinding flash. The creature also had a camera for each eye. When he took snapshots, it was like being hit with a bolt of lightning.

Next came a skeleton in a red beret. *"Bonjour!"* he said as he jumped down from the mirror.

"Jacques La Lean!" said Lydia with a relieved sigh. It was nice to see a familiar face. "I didn't know you were on the tour!"

"I have always wanted to zee how you live up here," explained Jacques. "So when Byetelzhooze told me about ze tour, I was—"

He didn't get to finish his sentence. Because just then a basketball came flying out of the mirror and knocked him on the head.

"Eazy, Basketball," Jacques said. "She's joost a little excited, Lydia, about ze tour."

Basketball's eyes gleamed. "That's right, just a little excited," the ball repeated in a high voice. "Hi, I'm Basketball." The ball flew into Lydia's arms.

There was a burst of smoke from the mirror. When the smoke settled, a vampire in a huge black cape appeared. He bared two huge white fangs.

"Cool," Lydia said.

"My name is not 'Cool,'" said the vampire with disgust. "My name is Count Fang. Is there a blood bank on the tour? I'm very thirsty."

Lydia wiped sweat from her brow. "We'll look for one. Okay, are we all here?"

"Now we are," said a muffled voice in the mirror. The mirror was filled with what looked like a mass of blue Jell-O. The Jell-O plopped onto the floor in a big pile. There was a strange slurping noise as the slime formed itself into a round shape with gloppy legs and arms. It slopped toward Lydia. It seemed to be looking at her, even though it had no face or eyes.

"I'm Blue Slime," said the jelly in a sad, gravelly voice. "Sorry I'm late. I was a little scared about traveling so far from home."

"Oh, don't worry," Lydia said. "There's nothing to be scared of in Peaceful Pines. Believe me, the people here are going to be scared of *you*."

"Really?" The Blue Slime seemed relieved. "Oh, thank you. I feel better already."

"Okay," Lydia said. "I guess we ought to get started."

The seven creatures all jumped up and down and chattered noisily with excitement.

"Sssssbbbb!" shushed Lydia. "Now listen, we better set a couple of rules so we all stay safe and sound. Rule number one. We're going to have be very quiet so we don't wake up anybody."

"QUIET!" roared Big Mouth.

"Rule number two," said Lydia, glaring at Big Mouth. "Everyone stick close by me and . . . um . . . do what I say, okay?"

"Okay," they all agreed. Big Mouth just shook his body, yes.

"Good. Well. Let's begin."

The seven tourists let out a scream of excitement. But they managed to stifle it before Lydia had to shush them again.

"This way." Lydia opened her door and tiptoed out. She started down the stairs and motioned for her tourists to follow her.

When they were safely outside the house, Lydia said, "Okay. Let's take a head count." She counted to seven. All clear.

Meanwhile, down in the Neitherworld, a line of monsters stretched as far as the eye could see. There were skeletons, hairy monsters, hairless monsters, giant bugs, tiny bugs, snakes, bats, and more. Many were carrying travel bags and cameras. The line led right into Beetlejuice's Roadhouse shack.

TWISTED TOURS INC.
SEE THE REAL WORLD
B

"Step right up. Don't be shy. See the sights, frights!" Beetlejuice barked into his megaphone. "That's right, only five hundred dollars for the greatest tour in the history of the Neitherworld. Sign up here!"

Then he turned off the megaphone and added, "Suckers!"

On top of the shack was a huge pink neon sign that blinked on and off "Twisted Tours, Inc."

Below that was a green neon globe of Earth and a red neon sign that read "See the *Real* World!"

Inside the Roadhouse were posters of the Grand Canyon, Mt. Rushmore, and Niagara Falls. "All For Only Five Hundred Smackers," said the sign underneath the posters. The line of monsters snaked all the way to a desk whose sign read "Twisted Tours, President."

"Where is he? I've been waiting for an hour already," complained the giant mosquito who was first in line.

"He's right here, kiddo," said Beetlejuice, as he raced inside and jumped behind the desk.

"Let me get this straight," said the mosquito, pressing her giant stinger against Beetlejuice's forehead. "I get to see all these places in one night?" The bug waved a wing at the posters. "And then I come back to the Neitherworld, right?"

"That's right," promised Beetlejuice. Then he

turned his back and snickered, "Except for the coming back part!"

"No fine print?" asked the mosquito, peering at the ghost.

"Fine print?" Beetlejuice laughed nervously. For he had written the details of his plan in barely readable type on the bottom of the posters. As the fine print explained, the Monster Across the Street had offered Beetlejuice $500 per monster if he could get rid of some of the Neitherworld's creatures and make the Neitherworld less crowded. Anyone going on a tour would leave the Neitherworld forever!

Luckily, the ghost's fine print was too fine for the mosquito to read. "All right," the mosquito said. "I'll go tonight." She opened her purse and started counting out the bills.

Beetlejuice turned back to the crowd with a big green-toothed smile. "Okay, tourists, have your money out and your visa books open," he yelled, "so I can stamp them." The crowd pushed forward, holding out a mass of bills and open visa books.

With a leering grin, he stamped each book "Approved For One-Way Travel—B.J."

He cackled happily. Why, at this rate, he'd have thousands of Neitherworld tourists ready for travel in no time.

CHAPTER FOUR

THE KISS OF DEATH

"NOW THIS IS MAIN STREET," Lydia told her travelers as they gathered on the sidewalk on Peaceful Pines' biggest street. "I know, it's pretty dinky, just ten stores, but—"

"SOUVENIRS!" bellowed Big Mouth.

"Hey, wait—guys!"

Lydia's entire tour group was running toward Bob's Odds 'n' Ends. Big Mouth and Blue Slime banged on the store window, chanting, "T-shirts! Postcards! Keychains! Knicknacks! Whatnots!"

But the store was locked. It *was* after midnight.

"Vat kind of lousy tour doesn't allow for souvenirs?" drawled Count Fang.

"Wait a minute!" said Lydia. "Easy now. I'll tell you what. How about we make this the *last* stop on the tour, so you don't have to carry the stuff everywhere? When we come back, Arthur can—"

But even as she spoke, Arthur was changing shape. He flew out of her hand, slipped into the lock, and opened the door to the store.

It was twenty minutes before Lydia's group came back out. Jacques La Lean was now wearing a T-shirt that read, "I Visited Peaceful Pines And All I Got Was This Lousy T-Shirt!" Blue Slime was wearing sunglasses, a Hawaiian shirt, and a straw hat. All the other tourists were carrying bags of film and candy and postcards. At Lydia's command, the group left money on the counter for everything they took.

A block later, Lydia said, "Okay, here's the first thing I wanted to show you." She was standing outside the brick building that housed Peaceful Pines' art museum.

"Cool!" said Basketball, peering at the building.

"How about a picture of all of us standing in front of it?" cried the Creature with a Thousand Eyes.

"No, no," Lydia said. "What I want to show you is inside the museum." But the tour group had already gathered around Lydia, posing for the snapshot. She felt the gloppy hand of Blue Slime slide onto her shoulder. Oh, please, don't let anyone wake up and look out their window, Lydia prayed to herself.

PEACEFUL PINES
ART MUSEUM
i visted Peaceful Pines and All i Got was this shirt
TOUR GUIDE
CANDY

"Say 'greasy grimy gopher guts,'" instructed Thousand Eyes.

"Greasy grimy gopher guts," said the group. There was a blinding flash of light. Thousand Eyes had snapped a thousand shots.

"All right," Lydia said. "Arthur? Could you get the lock?"

The little key fit himself into the lock in the museum's front door, changed shape, turned, and they were in.

"Ooh la la," said Jacques La Lean, pointing at a painting of a woman. "She is zo out of shape."

"Yes, well," Lydia blushed. "That painting was done by a man named Josef von Blubber a long time ago. Back then, you were supposed to weigh more if you wanted to look pretty."

"Beautiful, beautiful," murmured Blue Slime, as he squished along through the museum.

"Let's stick together," Lydia called to her group. But Blue Slime had found a George Gloppy painting from the artist's famous Blue Goo period and he refused to budge. "I could look at this all night," he said.

Big Mouth popped forty chocolate toffee candies into his mouth at one time and said, "I DON'T GET IT!"

"Easy on the candy," Lydia warned. "You'll get sick. Follow me—"

Grandmother and Count Fang had found a painting that looked just like Grandmother. "Can you believe it, Lydia?" Grandmother said, posing in front of the painting. "It's me!"

"Nope. It's *Vistler's Mother,*" Count Fang said, reading the label underneath the painting. "Boy, I vish *I* could vistle," he added. He blew air through his fangs.

Lydia chuckled and said, "Okay, let's go." She headed into the next room.

"It's not *Vistler's Mother,*" Grandmother insisted. "It's me. Here, look." She made herself as thin as paint and placed herself in the picture's rocking chair. She pushed with her forty hairy toes and started to rock. "See?"

But Count Fang had moved on as well, still trying to "vistle." Grandmother tried to hop down from the painting. She didn't want to lose the others. But she was stuck.

"Uh-oh," she said. "Lydia? Lydia?!"

But Lydia was now leading the tour group back out of the museum, and turning off the lights.

"Mon Dieu!" gasped Jacques La Lean, lifting a barbell. "Just look at zis equipment!"

They were in the Iron Man Health Spa on Orchard Street. "Please stick close together, everyone," Lydia called.

But Jacques had spotted what looked like a small set of stairs in the owner's private office. He hurried over. Star Stairs, said the machine's label, The Ultimate Workout. He climbed aboard, and turned the switch to on. Soon he was climbing stairs over and over. "Oo, zis is zo good for ze legs!"

Then he heard Lydia yelling that the tour was moving on. He reached down and turned the switch to off. But the stairs climbed faster. And faster. Jacques couldn't get off!

By the time Lydia's tour reached City Hall, Jacques's Star Stairs monitor read "3,000,000 Stairs Climbed!" And Jacques was still climbing.

Big Mouth had swallowed his last piece of Chocolate Oooze. He wandered into one of the rooms in City Hall, found a huge soft leather chair, and climbed in. He belched. Then he fell sound asleep. Still, Lydia kept moving on.

Blue Slime kept up with the tour until they stopped at the water company. Lydia was pointing out the vats that cleaned Peaceful Pines' water supply. Blue Slime took a step closer so he could see better, and slipped down a drain. He gurgled once and was gone.

Basketball stayed close to Lydia until they got to Miss Shannon's School for Girls. Then she stayed behind in the gym and tried to strike up a conversation with twenty other basketballs. But they wouldn't say a word. When the lights flicked out, she was locked inside.

Thousand Eyes, meanwhile, got locked in Ollie's Optical Store, where he was trying on glasses.

By the time Lydia arrived at the Peaceful Pines Cinema, she was exhausted. She looked at her watch: two in the morning! She had packed a lot into her tour and she was glad it would soon be over. This seemed like an awful lot of trouble, even for a CD player.

"This is the last stop on the tour," she said, looking up at the movie marquee. "This is a movie theater. As you can see, they're showing *Vampira and the Kiss of Death*. It's pretty good. I've seen it"—Lydia yawned out the last words—"s-e-v-e-n t-i-m-e-s. Excuse me."

She put her hand over her mouth. Then she turned around to face her group.

Instantly she was wide awake! The only tourist left was Count Fang.

"Rats and bats! She is beautiful!" gasped the Count. He moved closer to the movie poster.

"Count Fang! Where is everybody?" shrieked Lydia.

"Who?"

"The group! Grandmother, Basketball—"

But the Count wasn't listening. He couldn't take his eyes off the picture of Vampira.

"Count Fang!" Lydia shook the vampire by the shoulders. "What happened to the other creatures?"

"Hey, Fang," said a snide little voice. It was the key in Lydia's hand. Arthur was gazing up at the poster with his beady little eyes. "This looks like a pretty good flick. Let's check it out, whadda ya say?"

"I say no!" Lydia said. "I need you to help me find everyone—and fast."

But the skeleton key wasn't listening. He was opening the movie theater's front door. "C'mon, Fang. You want to meet Vampira, right?"

Lydia lunged for the Count's cape. But he pulled it behind him with a flourish and rushed into the theater.

"NO!" yelled Lydia. "ARTHUR!"

Arthur was moving fast. He threw himself into the lock on the inside of the theater door. Lydia grabbed the doorknob with all the strength she had left. But Arthur turned himself just in time.

The door locked.

Lydia had just lost her last two tourists.

CHAPTER FIVE

THREE THOUSAND AND TWO ONE-WAY TICKETS

"CHARLES?" Delia nudged her husband. "Charles!"

"Mmm . . . what, dear?"

"Charles, I think there are hundreds of monsters walking past our bedroom."

Charles sat up in bed. "Hmm? What? I can't see any monsters."

"They're right there." Delia pointed.

"I still don't see anything," insisted Charles. Delia looked at her husband. She pulled off his black sleep mask. "There!"

She was pointing at a six-foot-tall orange worm. The worm waved back at her. Then he yelled, "Hey, guys! I found some people!" Soon their bed was surrounded by monsters, all pointing at them and snapping pictures.

"Honey," said Charles, "I think there are monsters in our bedroom, taking pictures of us."

"That's what I've been trying to tell you," Delia said.

"Do you know what that means?" Charles asked her.

"What?"

"It means we're having a nightmare."

"Oh."

Charles smiled and gave his wife a peck on the cheek. "Goodnight, dear."

Mr. and Mrs. Deetz put their sleep masks back on and went back to sleep.

Meanwhile, down in the Neitherworld, the Monster Across the Street was returning from a late-night jog with his pet dog, Poopsie. Suddenly, he stopped short. So did Poopsie.

They had to. Their house was surrounded by so many creatures they couldn't take another step.

"HEY! WHAT'S GOING ON HERE!" roared the Monster.

"Looks like the crowd is trying to get to Beetlejuice's Roadhouse," observed Poopsie.

"What?" rasped the Monster. "I hired him to get the crowds out of our part of the Neitherworld, not bring them in!" He started forward, yelling, "BEETLEJUICE!"

Home
Sweet

As the Monster moved forward he picked up and glared at every creature that blocked his path. "Not Beetlejuice," he said to himself, throwing a giant bird over his head. Every now and then, the Monster paused to roar, "I'M GOING TO GET YOU, BEETLEJUICE!" His huge voice blew away twenty more creatures. Then he went back to throwing the beings over his head.

He and Poopsie finally made it inside the Roadhouse. The Monster picked up another creature. This one had yellow hair and a striped suit and was holding a huge sack of ticket stubs. In his rage, the creature didn't recognize the ghost. "Not Beetlejuice," said The Monster Across the Street. And over his head Beetlejuice went.

"But that *was* Beetlejuice," said Poopsie, looking up at his master.

"It was?"

The Monster Across the Street turned and saw Beetlejuice. He was back on his feet now, and running away. The Monster stretched out one long hairy arm. Beetlejuice ran right into his hand. The monster reeled him in.

"So my little traitor," said the Monster. "You have failed again!"

"I haven't. My plan is working beautifully," said Beetlejuice. His green teeth were chattering so hard they kept flying out of his mouth. "You see all these creatures? They're all going on a trip. A *one-way* trip out of the Neitherworld. Get it? They'll never be coming back. It's sheer genius."

"All I know is what I see," growled the Monster. "I can't even get into my house! Okay, Poopsie." He let go of the werewolf's leash. "Sic 'em."

"NO!" Beetlejuice started running again. Poopsie's paws scrambled on the floor as he struggled to get a grip. Then he shot off like a cannon.

"HEEEELLLLLPPPP!" cried Beetlejuice, trying to run faster.

But Poopsie was gaining on him. He opened his jaws wide. His sharp teeth gleamed in the darkness. Then he snapped his jaws shut.

That was the moment when Lydia discovered her tourists were missing. "BEETLEJUICE! BEETLEJUICE! BEETLEJUICE!" she yelled, clutching her head.

Poopsie snapped his jaws shut with all his might. But all he bit was his own tongue. Beetlejuice was gone.

"*Doggone* it, am I ever glad you called!" Beetlejuice said, slapping Lydia on the back. "I was about to get wolfed down for dinner."

"That's nothing compared to what I'm going to do to you," Lydia screamed. "Remember how you said nothing was going to go wrong?"

"Did I say that?" Beetlejuice asked innocently.

"Well, take a good look around."

Beetlejuice swiveled his head around in a complete circle.

"See any tourists?" asked Lydia. "No, you don't, because they're all—"

Lydia stopped cold.

A steady stream of creatures was now wandering down the street.

"See," said Beetlejuice. "There are plenty of tourists."

"Beetlejuice," whispered Lydia, who was now breaking out in a cold sweat. "What have you done?"

"What have I done? I've struck gold." The ghost's head turned to gold. He hit it. "Lyds, I'm rich. With the money I've made tonight, you can buy a whole funeral parlor, never mind just one stupid set of songs and a CD player."

"Beetlejuice, send these creatures home this instant. All of them." Lydia was on the verge of hysterics.

"Oh, come on, babes. They're on vacation."

"*NOW*, Beetlejuice, if you know what's good for you!"

Pictures of beetles swam in the ghost's eyes. He licked his lips with his striped tongue. "I know exactly what's good for me!"

"I'm not fooling!" Lydia said, grabbing the spirit by the collar. "Send them back this instant!"

"Uh, Lyds, well, see, that's something I've been meaning to talk to you about. You remember that spell you said?"

"Yes," Lydia replied through clenched teeth.

"Well, you might say it *spells* trouble."

Lydia barely stifled a scream. "How?"

"You let the creatures come whenever they pleasa, right? But you didn't say anything about when they had to leava."

"You didn't tell me to!" said Lydia.

Beetlejuice shrugged. "My mistake!"

"Your mistake?!!"

"I'm only human."

"You're *not* human!"

"There you have it." Beetlejuice pulled out his sack, which was bulging with ticket stubs. He pulled out one of the stubs to show her. "See? One-way."

Lydia turned pale as all the blood drained out of her face. "So when will they leave?" she asked in a quiet voice.

"Never," said Beetlejuice.

"Never?" Lydia mouthed the word faintly.

Beetlejuice nodded. "But here's the good news. I've got three thousand and two of these stubs. Do you know how much money that means I've—"

Lydia stepped on Beetlejuice's toes as hard as she could. "I don't care how many stubs you have," she said as the ghost yowled in pain. "We've got to get these creatures to go back home, and we've got to do it fast. Before anyone wakes up."

Lydia tried to pull herself together. She looked at her watch. Two thirty A.M. They had only a few hours. "Okay, Beetlejuice. You got us into this. Now how are you going to get us out?"

"Oh, that's simple," said Beetlejuice. "But I don't want to do it because—"

"I *don't* want to hear about the money. Now how do we do it?"

"All we have to do is convince each and every creature to go back to the Neitherworld of his or her own free will." Beetlejuice smiled.

Lydia stared at him in amazement. "What's simple about that?"

Beetlejuice thought for a moment. "You know, Lyds. You're absolutely right. There's nothing simple about it. In fact, I think it's impossible!"

He cackled. Then he started to run. Because Lydia was chasing him, and she was *mad*.

CHAPTER SIX

LET SLEEPING GHOSTS LIE

"WHERE COULD THEY HAVE ALL GONE?" moaned Lydia. She was standing on top of Pine Mountain, which overlooked Peaceful Pines. So far she and Beetlejuice hadn't been able to find a single tourist. She looked at her watch. "Four o'clock! It's almost morning!"

Beetlejuice's white stripes and purple shirt turned to black. He sobbed into his hanky. Tears poured out of his eyes. "I'm in mourning, already," he said.

"Now listen to me," Lydia said, grabbing the ghost by the nose. "We have got to get those creatures back to the Neitherworld fast, or we'll both really have something to cry about. Now why don't we retrace my steps?"

Beetlejuice shrugged and bent down to examine the footprints Lydia's sneakers had left in the dirt. He started painting a red outline around each footprint.

"BEETLEJUICE!" screamed Lydia. "THIS IS SERIOUS! WE'VE GOT TO HURRY!"

"Oh. Why didn't you say so?" The ghost snapped his red-tipped fingers. A rocket appeared. "Hop aboard."

Lydia got on the rocket and the pair blasted off. They blasted straight to Lydia's first stop on the tour—Bob's Odds 'n' Ends. They also blasted right through the glass storefront window. Then they blasted right out the back wall of the building.

"I didn't see any tourists, did you?" Beetlejuice asked Lydia, as they continued to rocket onward, zooming off into the sunset. "But hey, I'm having a *blast*."

"BEETLEJUICE! STOP THIS THING RIGHT NOW!"

The rocket screeched to a halt in midair. They began to plummet downward. Lydia closed her eyes. They crashed through the ceiling of the art museum. Luckily, they landed right in the middle of a huge abstract sculpture that was made out of pillows."Wow!" said Beetlejuice. "That landing was a real work of art."

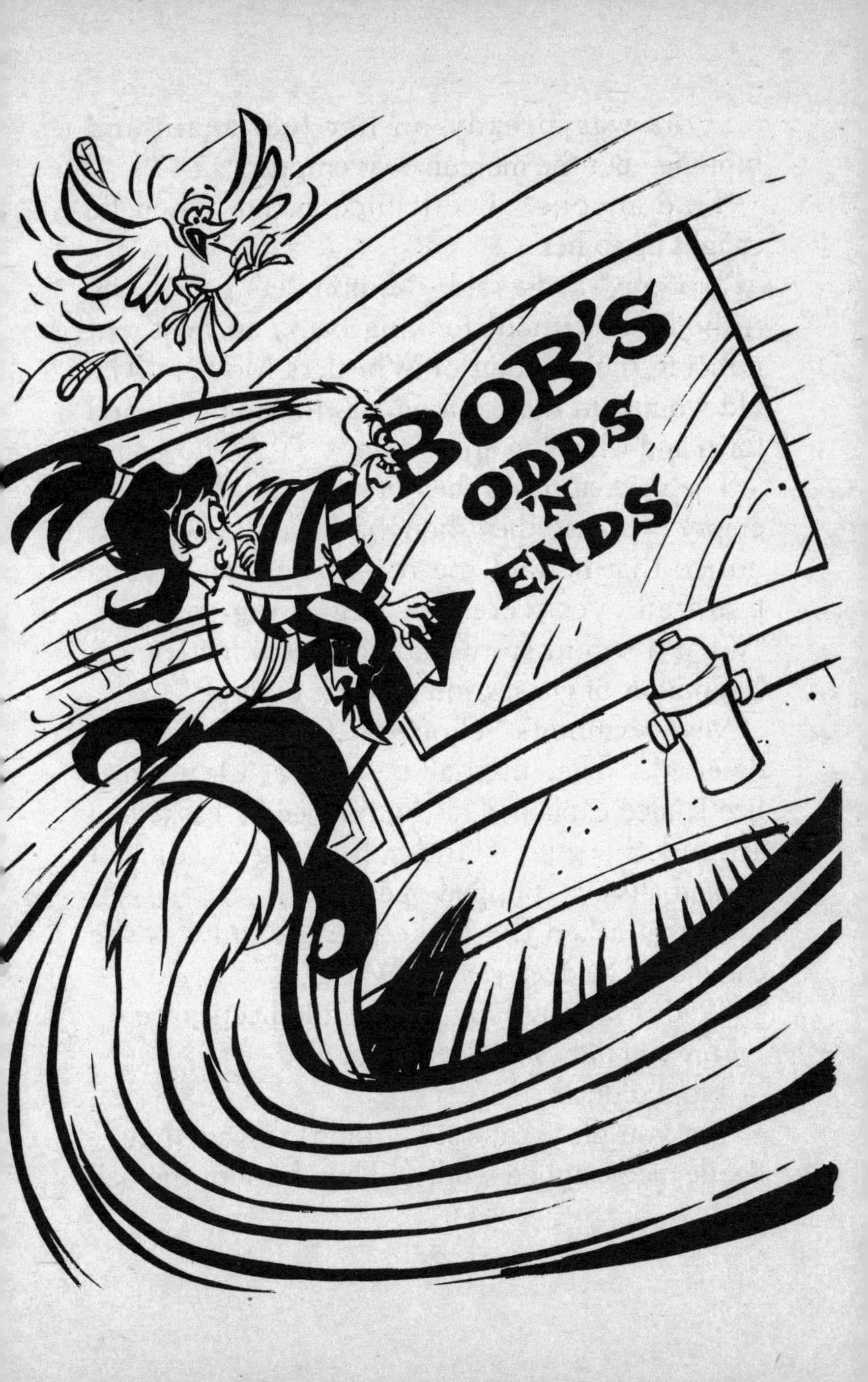
BOB'S
ODDS
'N
ENDS

Lydia was already on her feet again and running. But the museum was empty.

"Find anyone?" Beetlejuice asked, when he caught up to her.

"No one," Lydia said. "C'mon, let's go." They rushed out without looking back, and without noticing the painting of Whistler's Mother. The old woman in the painting was rocking back and forth and whistling up a storm.

The next stop was the optical store. It was also empty. At least, they thought it was. Lydia didn't notice that behind the pairs of glasses several hundred eyes were just beginning to open. "What a stupid store," commented Beetlejuice. "Hundreds of glasses and nothing to drink."

Miss Shannon's School for Girls was equally deserted. "They must all be hiding. Or resting," Beetlejuice explained, as he bounced a basketball around the gym. Under his fingers, one of Basketball's eyes popped open.

"Huh?" asked the Basketball groggily, as she came out of a deep sleep. "Whazzat?"

"I didn't say anything," Lydia told Beetlejuice.

"Yes you did," said Beetlejuice.

"No, I didn't!"

"But you did. You said, 'I didn't say anything.'" Beetlejuice laughed wildly. Then he shot the ball

all the way across the gym toward the opposite basket.

He missed. Basketball crashed into the bleachers with a groan. But Lydia and Beetlejuice were too far away to hear her.

"It's very late," Beetlejuice said with a yawn, as the two friends staggered through the main square of Peaceful Pines. "Don't you think we should continue our search tomorrow?"

"By tomorrow they'll be searching for *me*," Lydia said, her voice cracking.

They sat down on a park bench, not far from where Beetlejuice had played the organ music for Lydia. That seemed like ages ago. And a much happier time. Why had she let herself get drawn into this? And all for $212.99!

Beetlejuice laid his head down on the bench and began to snore loudly. He snored so loudly that Lydia didn't hear the bench, which had begun to snore as well. And she was so tired that she didn't notice the bench had hair on its legs and toes on every foot. She and Beetlejuice were sitting on top of one of the three thousand and two escaped creatures and they didn't even know it!

Lydia stretched and let out a gigantic yawn. "I've got to do something to get us out of this," she said sleepily.

She slumped further down on the bench. "But what?"

Her head began to drop forward.

For the moment, it seemed, there was absolutely nothing to be done.

Her head now rested on her chest. She struggled to keep her eyes open.

And then, her eyes closed.

It's probably a good idea for me to get some rest, she thought.

She suspected that she would need all of her strength for tomorrow.

She was right.

CHAPTER SEVEN

ATTACK OF THE NEITHERWORLD TOURISTS!

AT 6:21 A.M. THE SUN BEGAN TO RISE over the sweet little town of Peaceful Pines.

At 7:34 A.M. the sky cleared. It was going to be another picture-perfect spring day.

At 8:00 A.M. the town square's water sprinklers slowly spun into motion, spraying the lawns with bright blue slime.

At 8:01 A.M. the slime splattered against one of the park benches. There were two people sleeping on that bench. One of them woke up.

"Beetlejuice!" said Lydia, poking the ghost. "Wake up. It's raining!"

"Oooh," said Beetlejuice, rubbing his eyes. "I was having a nightmare. I dreamed I was a ghost."

"You are a ghost," Lydia told him. "And you just woke up to a real nightmare. We've got three thousand and two—"

The next wave of blue slime hit them in the face. "Why is it raining when the sun is shining and the sky is blue?" Beetlejuice wondered.

"It's the sprinklers," Lydia said. "But the water is blue!"

"And slimy," said Beetlejuice, happily smacking his lips as he tried to catch more of the water.

"Slimy?" asked Lydia with mounting horror. "Oh, no! Beetlejuice, I must have lost the Blue Slime at the water company. You don't think he could have—"

"Dissolved? You're right! You've *dissolved* the mystery!"

"Let's go!" Lydia yelled as she started to run. Beetlejuice ran after her.

When Lydia and Beetlejuice arrived at the water company, there was already a huge crowd. Police cars were parked out front, their lights flashing.

"It's sabotage!" a man was telling the police.

"When we catch the creeps who did this, we'll throw 'em in jail for life!" the police captain growled.

Lydia and Beetlejuice tiptoed away.

"I'm doomed," Lydia said.

"Now don't get blue," joked the ghost.

Lydia just sighed.

Meanwhile, at the Deetz house, Lydia's father was about to brush his teeth. Then he turned on the tap and dropped the brush in shock as blue ooze burbled out. "Honey?" he called. "I think we better call the plumber."

Across town, the owner of Ollie's Opticals arrived for work and opened up his store. He was greeted by a blinding light, as if a thousand flashbulbs had just popped at once. He squinted as he tried to make out what had happened.

"Noooo!" said a voice in the dark store. "You've got to smile! Now say 'grubby grody gizzard goo.'"

The store owner wasn't saying a word. But his eyes were *wide* open as he fell flat on his face.

At the town library, Mrs. Grizzle was working at the reference desk when she heard a piercing scream. She looked up. And up. And up. In front of her was a family of eight-foot tall butterflies. They were each carrying a huge net.

"Excuse me," said the mother butterfly in a soft voice. "Where would we find books on human collecting?"

Lydia and Beetlejuice were running past the library when Mrs. Grizzle came racing out.

"Gotcha!" yelled the gigantic butterfly who was running behind her. She caught the librarian in her net.

Before Lydia could do anything, the butterflies flapped their wings and flew away, carrying Mrs. Grizzle with them. Lydia could hear them giggling with excitement.

Meanwhile, in the town square, the Bench Beings were whizzing people around the park like bumper cars. Back at the Iron Man Health Spa, Jacques La Lean was *still* climbing stairs on the Star Stairs machine. The machine had been going faster and faster all night. The monitor now read "Congratulations! 20 Trillion Stairs Climbed!" And as a skeleton, Jacques couldn't afford to lose any more weight.

"Pleeze, somebody help me," said Jacques helplessly.

Just then, the lights clicked on. Harry Boron, the musclebound owner of the spa, walked into the main exercise room. Then he noticed the skeleton who was riding the Star Stairs in his private office. Jacques waved.

"Bonjour, monsieur. I can't zeem . . . to stop ze machine. I wonder if perhaps you might—"

Harry started to sway. Then it all went black, and he toppled down.

A moment later, the Star Stairs machine began to wheeze in a funny way. Then it made a grinding sound. All at once—*BOINK!*—something snapped. The Star Stairs machine came to an abrupt halt.

"Whew!" Jacques said breathlessly. "Now zat was some workout!"

Jacques wandered out into the exercise room. The members of Harry Boron's first aerobics class were just arriving. When they saw Jacques, they tried to do the hundred-yard dash for the door. But the door locked before anyone could escape.

"Not so fast," said a snide little voice on the other side of the door.

"Arthur!" Jacques called. "Is zat you? Let us out!"

"Yeah! Let us out!" screamed the aerobics class.

The key just snickered. "But you haven't exercised yet," said Arthur with a laugh. "And exercise is . . . key!"

With that the little key was off and running.

"Vampira and the Kiss of Death," said Beetlejuice outside the theater. He and Lydia were back where they started. "Sounds like a good flick," he mused, flicking his tongue to catch a fly.

It was noon, and they had been running from

one crisis to another all morning. So far they hadn't convinced a single tourist to go home.

"Tickets, please," said the usher, as Lydia charged into the theater.

"Oh, I don't want to see the movie," Lydia said breathlessly.

"Sure," said the usher. "And I was born yesterday."

"So was I," said the yellow-haired baby in Lydia's arms. Lydia stared down at him in astonishment. "It'll save money on tickets," the Beetlejuice baby told her with a wink.

Lydia bought two tickets—one adult, one child—and rushed inside.

The movie had just begun. There were only a few people in the audience. Count Fang was *not* one of them.

"Fang's not here," Lydia said, coming out into the lobby.

"So?" Beetlejuice said. "Let's watch the movie."

"Are you crazy? We've got a little problem to take care of, remember?"

Suddenly, a scream of delight was heard throughout the theater. "Vampira!"

Lydia whirled around and faced the movie screen. The actress in the picture was growing fangs. "My name is Vampira. And now I vill give you the kiss of death!"

"VAMPIRA!" screamed the voice again. It was coming from behind the screen. "I'VE FOUND YOU AT LAST!" The screen ripped open as Count Fang clawed and bit his way toward the huge figure of Vampira. "Vampira, I've come for you. You vill love me too, I know it!"

The few people who were in the audience were now screaming and running. The projectionist ran, too. The screen went dark. Beetlejuice and Lydia raced through the dark theater searching for Count Fang. But he had escaped again.

"Hey, check that out," said Beetlejuice, as they came out of the theater. He pointed a finger at the gym across the street. "That gym instructor is working those people to the bone!"

Lydia looked through the windows. The second floor aerobics class was nothing but skeletons doing jumping jacks. "Jacques!" she whispered.

Lydia and Beetlejuice raced over to the gym. But when they got upstairs, they found the exercise room locked. Jacques appeared at the glass door. "Lydia! Byetelzhooze! I am zo glad to zee you!"

"Can the sweet talk, you nut," said Beetlejuice, shaping his head into a can of nuts. "Open up."

"But zat is joost the thing. Leetle Arthur has locked us all in."

"Stand back!" Beetlejuice commanded. "I know exactly what to do." He turned his entire body into a stick of dynamite and lit the fuse.

KABOOOOMMMM!!! The explosion knocked Beetlejuice senseless. But it didn't damage the door one bit.

Then Lydia noticed the button on the door's handle. She pressed on it and the button popped out. The door clicked open. "I still think I had a dynamite idea," said Beetlejuice, as he put himself back together.

Twenty people looking like skeletons in aerobics clothes raced past them, screaming. Lydia walked into the exercise room, where disco music played on the radio.

"Boy," said Jacques. "Zose students did not want to get into shape at all. I had to be very firm with them. What ees wrong, Lydia? You look sad."

"Jacques, if I asked you a very important favor, you'd do it for me, wouldn't you?" Lydia asked desperately, batting her eyes to look helpless.

"But of course," said Jacques. "For my friend, Lydia, anything at all."

"Then go back to the Neitherworld. The tour is over. *Please.*"

"Anything at all," said Jacques. "Exzept for zat. You zee, they have so much amazing equipment in this gym. I want to try the rowing machine next!" The skeleton ran across the room and started rowing.

Lydia sighed. "Well, Beetlejuice, there's one good thing."

"What's that?"

"Things can't get any worse."

Just then, static came over the gym's loudspeakers. "And now," said the radio announcer, "we interrupt our broadcast with this terrible news. As weird as this day has been so far, it is now getting worse."

"I guess I was wrong. What now?" Lydia asked.

"This just in. Big butterflies are collecting our townspeople! And giant birds are snatching our cars! They seem to be making a big stack of the cars just outside town. It appears they're gathering material for constructing their giant nests!"

Lydia and Beetlejuice ran to the window. A huge green bird flew by carrying a car in its beak.

"It's the Flying Dirty Birdies," said Beetlejuice.

"They've got Mrs. Clarkson," gasped Lydia, as she recognized the car's terrified driver.

"And now," said the radio announcer, "here's Jerry Ball with sports. Jerry, I understand you actually have some good news for us."

"That's right, Lou. There's a girl-boy basketball game in progress right now at Miss Shannon's School for Girls. And I want to tell you, the Shannon Shooters are having a field day against Mr. Bannon's boys team. I mean, Lou, the shots these girls are making. The ball just seems to fly out of their hands and head for the basket. At the half, the score is 6,282 for the girls and 0 for the boys. This is some basketball game!"

"Basketball!" said Lydia. "So that's where she went!"

"I'll drive!" announced Beetlejuice, turning himself into a car. Lydia scrambled on board.

They tried to drive down Main Street but got caught in bumper-to-bumper traffic. Panicked townspeople clogged the streets, trying to escape. Then a motorcade zoomed by, the other way.

The motorcade was led by twenty policemen on motorcycles. They were followed by a long black limo. Inside the limo was none other than the Mayor of Peaceful Pines.

The limo pulled up at City Hall, and the Mayor got out. Reporters were everywhere, flashing pictures.

"What are you going to do about the Dirty Birdies?" called one of the reporters.

"Is the blue slime safe to drink?"

"Isn't it time to call in the National Guard?"

"I'll answer all your questions at my press conference!" shouted the Mayor. The reporters surged after him as he made his way inside.

As soon as the Mayor entered the room, the TV cameramen all started their cameras rolling. Bright lights shone down on the Mayor's high-backed leather chair.

And then, just before the Mayor reached his desk, the leather chair swiveled around.

Sitting on the chair was a giant pair of red lips with tiny eyes, hands, and feet!

The lips opened. "WHAT'S GOING ON HERE?!!!" roared Big Mouth.

"I . . . I'm . . . having a press conference," mumbled the frightened Mayor.

"WHO ARE YOU?" Big Mouth demanded. "AND WHY DID YOU WAKE ME UP?"

"I . . . I'm . . . I'm the Mayor of Peaceful Pines. And who, I might ask, are you?"

The microphones were on. Big Mouth's huge voice was bigger than ever. And his answer to the Mayor could be heard all over town. Beetlejuice and Lydia screeched to a halt when they heard it.

"MY NAME IS BIG MOUTH," Big Mouth bellowed. "AND I AM THE NEW MAYOR OF PEACEFUL PINES!"

CHAPTER EIGHT

BIG MOUTH CALLS A MEETING

"TURN AROUND!" SAID LYDIA.

Beetlejuice took his hands off the wheel and turned around. "You know," he cackled, "this makes it kind of hard to see where I'm going."

"Turn the *car* around!" Lydia corrected herself. She covered her eyes. They were about to hit a tree. She waited for the crash.

It didn't come. When she took her hands off her eyes, she saw the tree jumping away. It shook a branch after them. "Watch where you're driving!" the tree yelled.

"Go home!" Lydia yelled back.

Beetlejuice spun the car in a circle and started driving back toward City Hall. The road back into town was empty. Everyone was going the other way.

Back at City Hall, the terrified Mayor of Peaceful Pines pushed his way out past the stunned reporters and headed for the pay phone. "Yes, Operator," he said. "Uh, connect me with General Bunstaff, would you? At the National Guard."

"Make way! Clear out! Outta our way!" Beetlejuice crashed his car up the steps of City Hall, through the doorway, and right into the front hall.

"We're here," Beetlejuice told Lydia. They hopped out of the car and raced into the Mayor's office.

"Mayor Big Mouth," a reporter was asking. "What do you plan to do about the blue slime crisis?"

"NONE OF YOUR BUSINESS!" shrieked Big Mouth.

"We've got to shut him up," Lydia told Beetlejuice.

"Piece of cake," said Beetlejuice. He snapped his fingers. Instantly the biggest piece of cake that Lydia had ever seen appeared beside her.

"Good thinking!" she said. From what she'd seen, Big Mouth couldn't resist sweets! She and Beetlejuice wheeled the cake forward. Lydia called out, "Mr. Mayor, your dessert has arrived."

"MY DESSERT?" blasted Big Mouth. When he saw the size of the cake, Big Mouth's tiny eyes grew wide. Then he began to open his huge mouth.

He opened wider. And wider.

And still it didn't seem as if he could fit the whole cake in his mouth.

"Lift," said Beetlejuice. He and Lydia strained and grunted as they struggled to lift the cake. They raised it over their heads.

"Push!" yelled Lydia. She and the ghost shoved the cake into the monster's huge mouth with all their might.

The cake fit snugly. "Ooomph," said Big Mouth in a tiny, muffled voice.

"I guess that about wraps up the press conference," said a reporter. The news people all drifted out as Big Mouth tried to chew.

"Beetlejuice," Lydia said, "we have another problem. One of the reporters told me that the real mayor's calling out the National Guard. Any minute there are going to be soldiers here, shooting at the Neitherworlders."

"That's bad," Beetlejuice agreed. He made a long face by pulling on his chin so that it stretched down to the ground.

"We've got to warn the monsters to go home,"

PRESS
MAYOR

Lydia went on. "Big Mouth," she said. "You've got the biggest mouth for miles. Tell everyone to go home!"

"Ha hoo hove hoo," Big Mouth said, his mouth full of cake.

"Beetlejuice!" Lydia whirled around to face the ghost. "We blew it. We've got to get that cake out of Big Mouth's mouth. Then we can use his huge voice to call a meeting."

"Okay, okay." The ghost rolled up his sleeves. "I guess I better just *plunge* in." Instantly his face began to widen and redden. His body got thinner and thinner. In seconds he had taken on the shape of a giant toilet plunger.

The plunger hurried all the way to the other side of the room, to get a running start. Then it ran forward, yelling *"KOWABUNGA!"*, and flung itself right into Big Mouth's mouth.

THWAP! The plunger stuck fast in the cake.

"Puh!" said the plunger in a muffled, quiet voice.

"What?" asked Lydia.

"Pull!" said the plunger.

Lydia pulled with all her might. The plunger wouldn't budge.

"Hey, this shot will be great for the *Neitherworld Times*!" Lydia heard a voice behind her say. It was the Creature with a Thousand Eyes. He snapped a thousand pictures right away.

"How about giving me a hand," said Lydia, grunting.

"You mean hands!" Thousand Eyes had a thousand tiny hands. He arranged them all over the plunger.

"Okay," said Lydia. "One, two, three, PULL!"

Thousand Eyes and Lydia strained hard. Until finally—

P L O P!

The plunger came loose.

Lydia and Thousand Eyes went flying backward, out of the room, and out of the building.

A moment after they landed, they were hit with a mass of white glop.

"Icing," said Lydia, licking her lips.

"Icing," agreed Delia Deetz, licking her lips at the same moment, three miles away. She and Charles were in the car. Charles was driving. They had been riding around town all day, frantically searching for Lydia. Now Charles turned on the windshield wipers to try to clear the sticky white goo. Delia started to scoop up the mess that had come through the windows.

"Don't eat it," he snapped. He stuck his head out the side window and peered cautiously upward. "It could be coming from those Dirty Birdies."

"No," Delia insisted. "It's icing. Look! The whole town is covered with it!"

It was true. All of Peaceful Pines had turned sticky white. And the stickiest, gooiest spot of all was City Hall. Lydia and Thousand Eyes slogged through the slop back into the mayor's office.

"MORE CAKE!" roared Big Mouth into the microphones.

"You'll get more cake, Big Mouth," promised Lydia, "just as soon as you deliver this message. 'Attention, all tourists—'"

"ATTENTION, ALL TOURISTS!" repeated Big Mouth.

"Go at once to the town square for a group meeting. The meeting will be led by your very own tour guide, Lydia."

"GO TO THE TOWN SQUARE FOR A MEETING," said Big Mouth. "RIGHT NOW."

"Close enough," Lydia said.

"NOW GIVE ME MY CAKE!"

"You'll get your cake right after the meeting."

"HEY! THAT'S NOT FAIR!" shouted Big Mouth. But he followed after her. So did Thousand Eyes, and so did Beetlejuice.

"Wait for me!" cried a tiny muffled voice. Lydia

reached down and felt around in the icing until she found Arthur. She stuck the sticky key in her pocket and hurried onward.

"Where is everybody?" Lydia wondered, as they sloshed through the white glop that covered the street.

"I guess the town is *desserted*," said Beetlejuice. He was riding on Big Mouth's back. The huge lips were bent low to the ground, sucking up the icing.

When they got to the town square, a crowd of monsters had already gathered. As Lydia elbowed her way through, she spotted a familiar black cape.

"Count Fang! We've been looking all over you." He grinned.

"You didn't say hello to me," said the painting on the count's left.

"Grandmother!" Lydia gasped.

Grandmother was still stuck in the painting. "Don't look so worried," she told Lydia. She wriggled her forty hairy toes. "The guards at the museum told me that now I'm priceless."

Lined up in the front three rows were all the Bench Beings. A group of monsters was trying to sit on them. But the benches threw them off. "We were here first," the benches cried. "Get behind us." Soon a fight broke out between the monsters and the benches.

"Stop!" cried Lydia from the podium Beetlejuice had produced for her. But it was no use. Another bench threw a monster into the crowd.

Suddenly, a skeleton reached out and lifted up all the fighting monsters in one bony hand, and all the benches in the other. "You better be quiet now, and no more of ze fighting!" he warned them.

"Jacques!" exclaimed Lydia. "Thank you! You saved the day!" He tipped his beret to her.

"Okay," shouted Lydia. "Is everybody here?"

"Looks like we're all present," said Beetlejuice wrapping himself with ribbon and a bow.

"But are we?" Lydia asked, not willing to make the same mistake she made earlier. She looked out at the sea of monster faces. There was no way to know.

"Time for a head count!" a high voice piped up.

"Basketball!" said Lydia as the ball bounced onto the stage."Follow the bouncing ball," cried Basketball. She bounced on Big Mouth and said "One."

"HEY!" yelled Big Mouth.

But Basketball was gone, bouncing on the heads of monster after monster, and calling out the numbers. "Three thousand and one!" cried the ball, bouncing on the last head.

"Are you sure?" asked Lydia. She frowned. They were short by one monster. Then it hit her. "Blue Slime! He's still in the water system." She looked out over the crowd of monster faces. There wasn't a moment to lose. "Well, we'll have to try to get him later." She turned to the huge red lips. Big Mouth!"

"CAKE!" Big Mouth roared back.

"As soon as the meeting is over. Now repeat everything I say. And I mean business! Ready?

"You all must go home right away," she began.

"YOU ALL MUST GIVE ME CAKE!" bellowed Big Mouth.

The crowd of monsters looked at each other strangely.

"Big Mouth," Lydia warned. "Do what I tell you or we'll—we'll—"

"Put you on a diet," said Beetlejuice.

Big Mouth trembled. "WE ALL MUST GO HOME RIGHT AWAY!" he roared at the crowd.

"The United States Army is going to be here any second," Lydia yelled.

"THE UNITED STATES SMARMY IS COMING!" repeated Big Mouth.

"You will all be killed."

"YOU WILL ALL BE KILLED."

The monsters all applauded loudly. "Sounds like fun!" called out a purple creature.

"More fun than I've had on this tour!" yelled an orange worm.

"We're not leaving till we see the Grand Canyon!" yelled a Dirty Birdy.

"Beetlejuice promised us we'd see Mt. Rushmore!" added a giant butterfly.

"And Niagara Falls!" added a Bench Being. "I still haven't seen Niagara Falls!"

"Beetlejuice," Lydia said, trying to remain calm. "Did you promise them they would see those places?"

"They were the only travel posters I could find," explained Beetlejuice with a shrug.

"I don't want to be an I-told-you-so," Lydia told Beetlejuice, "but haven't I told that you shouldn't lie to your customers?" Beetlejuice hung his head.

Lydia turned back to the crowd. She cleared her throat. And she tried one last time.

She pleaded. She begged. She gave the most moving speech she had ever given in her life.

When she was done, she wiped a tear from her eye, and said, "Now will you go?"

Thousands of monster heads turned this way

and that. The monsters all stared at one another, as if they were thinking it over. Then they shouted back at once:

"WE CAN'T HEAR YOU!"

The ground began to tremble. The podium shook.

"Beetlejuice," Lydia said, turning pale. "I think the army is here."

But it wasn't the army.

It was one last tourist.

"BEETLEJUICE!" yelled a voice that was even louder than Big Mouth's.

In the crowd, three thousand and one heads turned to see who was coming.

Up on stage, Beetlejuice had already seen who it was. He knew he hadn't sold a ticket to this guy!

The ground was still shaking.

And so was Beetlejuice. But now Beetlejuice was shaking with fear.

CHAPTER NINE

FRIGHT FIGHT

"BEETLEJUICE!" THE NEW TOURIST ROARED AGAIN. He had brown fur and a giant mouth in the middle of his chest.

"Tell me that's not the Monster Across the Street," Beetlejuice begged Lydia.

"It's the Monster Across the Street," snickered Arthur, from inside Lydia's pocket.

"I asked you not to tell me that," Beetlejuice shrieked, getting hysterical.

"DO YOU KNOW WHAT I'M GOING TO DO TO YOU?" the Monster Across the Street bellowed. He was making his way slowly toward the stage, pushing monsters out of his way.

"Is it something nice?" Beetlejuice asked sweetly.

"WRONG!" shouted the Monster Across the Street.

"Wrong," repeated Beetlejuice, as he turned into a host on a game show. He pulled a mike out of the sky and said, "But you still get our second prize, which is a home version of our game. And now, we've got to *break* for a commercial!"

Beetlejuice broke into a hundred pieces and each piece started to run. But a giant brown hand came down and scooped up all the pieces at once, squeezing them back into one.

Beetlejuice slithered free and hid in the crowd.

"COME OUT HERE, YOU SLIMY COWARD!" roared the Monster. "YOU BROKE YOUR PROMISE, AND NOW I'M GOING TO BREAK YOU."

"What promise?" Lydia asked him.

"He promised he would straighten up the Neitherworld," the Monster explained. "Get rid of some of these ghouls. I hired him to do a job and now he's going to pay!"

Lydia's face turned red with anger. "So that's why he gave them all one-way tickets!" she fumed. "And why he made me say that special spell. It wasn't a mistake after all!"

"B-b-b-but I kept my promise," Beetlejuice was telling the Monster. "Just look around you. Look at all the creatures I got rid of."

"Yeah," said the Monster. "But there's thousands MORE where these came from. And they're ALL STANDING outside YOUR HOUSE. And do you know WHERE YOUR HOUSE IS?"

"Is that a trick question?" Beetlejuice asked.

"IT'S RIGHT ACROSS THE STREET FROM MINE!"

The Monster reached his big paw into the crowd and made a swipe at Beetlejuice.

"Leave him alone!" shouted Lydia.

"Hey, thanks, kid," called Beetlejuice, as he crawled through the legs of a dragon. "You're a true friend."

"Go fight him down in the Neitherworld," Lydia added, feeling a bit guilty about saying it.

"I take it back," Beetlejuice said. He was now hiding behind a bunch of fat-looking monsters with big sticky fingers.

"Hey, looky here," said the ghost. "If it isn't my old friends, the Greedy Grabbers! You wouldn't mind helping me out here, wouldya? Maybe help me fight him? You know, thirty against one, that kind of thing?

They looked at him blankly.

"Look," he continued desperately. "I pulled a rotten stunt, I know. The thing is, I was greedy. You can understand that, can't you, guys?"

The Greedy Grabbers all nodded eagerly. Then they started yelling, "Tickets here, on sale now. It's the fright fight of the century!"

The monsters all formed a circle. Ticket sales were taking off. Beetlejuice tried to escape again. But one of the Greedy Grabbers caught him.

"C'mon, Beetlejuice. We're trying to help you out. If you win, you get some of the money. If you lose . . . well, you're dead. But, then, you already are dead. So what do you really have to lose?" The Grabber slapped his knee and broke into laughter.

Beetlejuice scowled. "Fine. Just watch this!"

Beetlejuice's muscles bulged until they popped right out of his suit. He swelled up till he was a hundred times his original size. He flexed a gigantic muscle.

But the Monster just laughed. Then he grabbed Beetlejuice. And threw him so high into the air that for a moment he was completely gone from the crowd's sight.

There was a loud whistling sound.

As the ghost plummeted downward, the whistling grew louder and louder.

Beetlejuice landed so hard he formed an enormous crater.

"It's the Grand Canyon!" yelled Thousand Eyes, snapping snapshots.

tickets for
the FRIGHT fight of the CENTURY

Grandmother whistled wildly. The crowd cheered with delight. All except Lydia, who ran to the hole. "Beetlejuice? Are you all right?"

There was no response. The Monster Across the Street peered down into the hole. "Here he is. Or part of him, anyway." He pulled out Beetlejuice's gigantic head.

"I don't normally give in so easily," Beetlejuice's head told the Monster. "But since we're all in a hurry, I'm just going to say 'mercy' and get this over with. 'Mercy.'"

The Monster now threw Beetlejuice's huge head with all his might. It smacked right into the side of Pine Mountain and stuck there, facing out.

"Hey!" yelled Count Fang. "It's Mt. Rushmore!"

The crowd cheered even more wildly than before.

"Okay," Lydia told the monsters. "Now you've seen the Grand Canyon and Mt. Rushmore. Please go home while you still can."

"What about Niagara Falls?!" yelled a Greedy Grabber.

Lydia didn't have time to answer. A strange rumbling sound was heard in the distance. Again the ground began to tremble.

"They're rolling in the tanks!" gasped Lydia. "Run for your lives!"

Just then the water company blew sky high.

CHAPTER TEN

THAR SHE BLOWS!

"THAR SHE BLOWS!" cried Beetlejuice's head, from Pine Mountain.

The crowd turned and saw—

A huge geyser of bright blue slime gushing out of the top of the water company.

All this time, the poor Blue Slime had been trapped in a vat at the water company. Through a strange chemical reaction, his slimy body had been multiplying. The pipes and vats just couldn't handle all the extra slime he was making.

Blue goop cascaded down, forming a blue river. The river was headed straight for the town square. It was out of control.

The crowd of monsters rushed out of the way of the river. Luckily, it flowed straight to the crater's edge. The blue slime poured and poured over the edge, falling with a crash.

"IT'S NIAGARA FALLS!" shouted Big Mouth.

The crowd went nuts, cheering and clapping.

"Now," pleaded Lydia, "you all got your wish. Please go home." She prayed the monsters would fall for this.

"She's right," said the Basketball. "We got our wish."

"She's right," agreed Grandmother.

"Wait a minute. We didn't see the *real* Niagara Falls," said Count Fang. "This tour was a rip-off!"

"The *tour* was a rip-off?" said Beetlejuice, putting his head back on. "How about the way that monster ripped off my head?"

Hundreds of hairy hands grabbed Beetlejuice. "Rip off," chanted the crowd. "We want our money back!"

"Well, okay, since you asked so nicely," said Beetlejuice as the monsters grabbed every last dollar out of the ghost's money sack. "Gee, I hate being broke," he complained, a crack zigzagging through his face.

"You're not broke. Here's your share of the fight ticket sales," said a Greedy Grabber. He handed Beetlejuice the cash.

"All right!" said Beetlejuice. "Two hundred and

twelve dollars and ninety-nine cents." The amount rang up in his eyes, and his stomach popped open like a cash register.

But Lydia was holding her hand out. "Which is exactly what you owe *me*, Beetlejuice."

"Owe, debt's right," said the ghost sadly.

"And *now, please*, everyone go home!" yelled Lydia.

"Go home?" cried the monsters. They began to talk among themselves. Finally they turned back to Lydia. "Go home!" cried the vast crowd. Lydia cheered.

She didn't cheer long. For now she heard what sounded like the beating of wings.

The sky darkened overhead. It was a vast fleet of army helicopters, coming right toward them. Their guns were ready.

Lydia closed her eyes. It was too late. They were all done for.

"SOUVENIRS!" yelled the Dirty Birdies, flapping their wings with excitement.

Within moments, the birds had caught all the helicopters in their claws and added them to their souvenir pile of cars outside of town. Pilots were parachuting down all over the place.

"We're saved!" cried Lydia.

"What a stroke of luck!" commented Beetle-

juice. He started doing the backstroke in the slime pool. Blue slime spurted out of his mouth like a fountain. Lydia breathed a sigh of relief.

Lydia lay on her bed, her headphones on her ears, a smile on her face. She was listening to her new CD player. Now playing—the World's Greatest Funeral Hits. She was humming along with a charming little organ number called "And You Thought I Was Rotten When I Was Alive!"

And best of all, Beetlejuice wasn't around to bother her. She was in such a good mood. She couldn't believe everything had worked out so beautifully. The tourists all went home happy. They had even cleaned up the mess they had made.

And Beetlejuice was able to get Blue Slime out of the vat at the water company.

"There's just one little problem," Blue Slime had told Beetlejuice. "Slime has another special property besides multiplying in water. It makes people forgetful. I'm afraid that by tomorrow, anyone who drank even a tiny bit of blue slime today won't remember any part of what happened."

Problem? What wonderful luck! Lydia was the only one in Peaceful Pines who remembered what had gone on!

Well, almost the only one. There was a knock at the door. Her father entered and started pacing up and down.

"Now, you're sure you don't remember any monsters?" Charles asked, for the hundredth time that day.

"None," Lydia said with a grin. "Are you sure you're all right?"

Charles wiped his face with his sleeve. "Well, I guess I really must have been dreaming. But it all seemed so real. You know, I was so scared I didn't have a bite to eat or drink all day." Charles kept pacing. "I don't know what's happening to me. I think I need a vacation."

Just then, the doorbell rang. Charles hurried downstairs as Lydia chuckled to herself. Poor dad!

Then she heard a familiar voice from downstairs.

And what she heard made her ponytail stand up even straighter than usual.

"Uh, Mr. Deetz," said the voice. "I'm from BJ Travel." The salesman let out a muffled laugh. "I wanted to tell you about a very special relaxing vacation tour we're offering. Here's the brochure. As you can see, you'll be staying at the lovely Neither hotel. . . ."